THIS WALKER BOOK BELONGS TO:

_____

_____

_____

First published 1983 by Julia MacRae Books
Published 1992 by Walker Books Ltd
87 Vauxhall Walk, London SE11 5HJ

This edition including CD published 2006 for Index

2 4 6 8 10 9 7 5 3 1

This book has been typeset in Palatino

Printed in China

British Library Cataloguing in Publication Data:
a catalogue record for this book is available from the British Library

ISBN-13: 978-1-4063-0538-8
ISBN-10: 1-4063-0538-3

www.walkerbooks.co.uk

GORILLA

Anthony Browne

WALKER BOOKS

AND SUBSIDIARIES

LONDON • BOSTON • SYDNEY • AUCKLAND

Hannah loved gorillas. She read books about gorillas, she watched gorillas on television, and she drew pictures of gorillas. But she had never seen a real gorilla.

Her father didn't have time to take her to see one at the zoo. He didn't have time for anything.

He went to work every day before Hannah went to school, and in the evening he worked at home.

When Hannah asked him a question, he would say, "Not now. I'm busy. Maybe tomorrow."

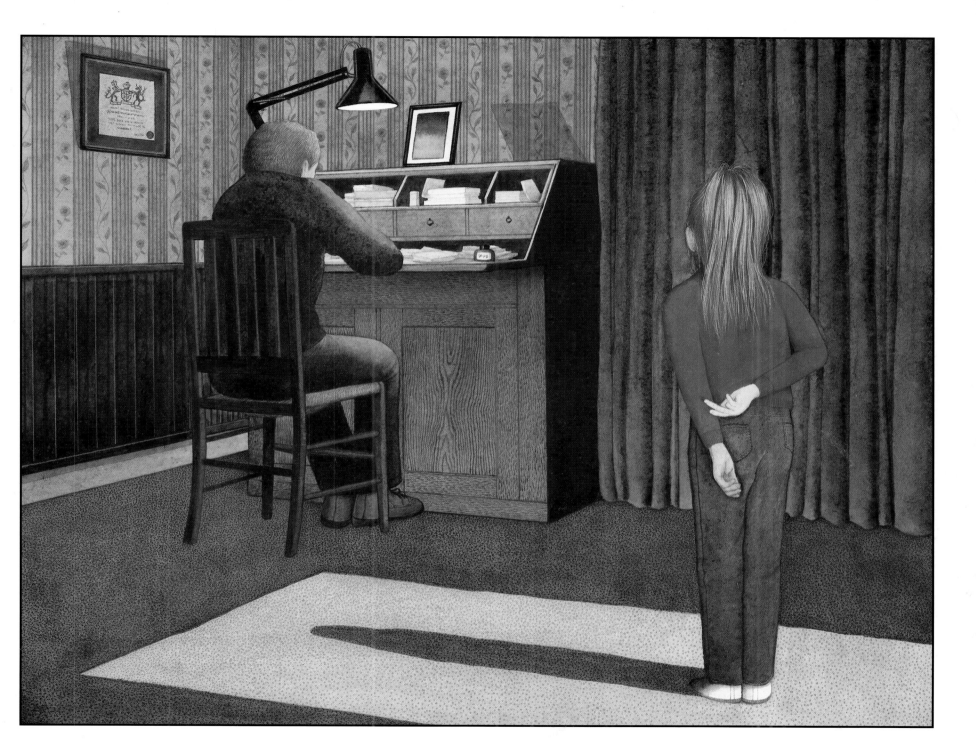

But the next day he was always too busy.
"Not now. Maybe at the weekend," he would say.
But at the weekend he was always too tired.
They never did anything together.

The night before her birthday, Hannah went to bed tingling
with excitement – she had asked her father for a gorilla!

   In the middle of the night, Hannah woke up and saw a very
small parcel at the foot of the bed. It *was* a gorilla, but
it was just a toy.

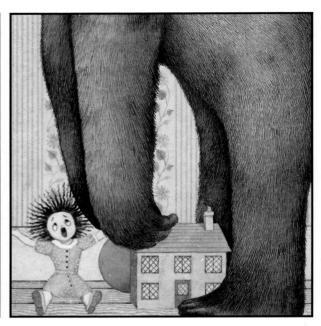

Hannah threw the gorilla into a corner with her other
toys and went back to sleep.
In the night something amazing happened.

Hannah was frightened. "Don't be frightened, Hannah," said the
gorilla, "I won't hurt you. I just wondered if you'd like to
go to the zoo."

The gorilla had such a nice smile that Hannah wasn't afraid.
"I'd love to," she said.

They both crept downstairs, and Hannah put on her coat. The
gorilla put on her father's hat and coat. "A perfect fit," he
whispered.

They opened the front door, and went outside.

"Come on then, Hannah," said the gorilla, and he gently lifted her up. Then they were off, swinging through the trees towards the zoo.

When they arrived at the zoo it was closed, and there was a high
wall all around. "Never mind," said the gorilla, "up and over!"
  They went straight to the primates. Hannah was thrilled.
So many gorillas!

The gorilla took Hannah to see the orang-utan, and a chimpanzee.
She thought they were beautiful. But sad.

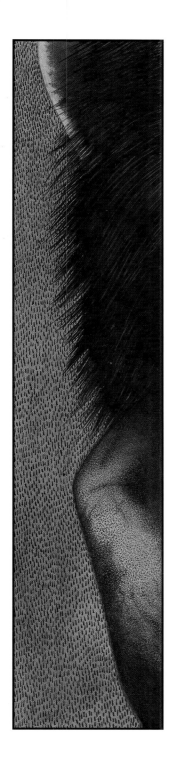

"What would you like to do now?" the gorilla asked. "I'd love
to go to the cinema," said Hannah. So they did.

Afterwards they walked down the street together. "That was wonderful,"
said Hannah, "but I'm hungry now."
"Okay," said the gorilla, "we'll eat."

"Time for home?" asked the gorilla.

Hannah nodded, a bit sleepily.

They danced on the lawn. Hannah had never been so happy.

"You'd better go in now, Hannah," said the gorilla. "See you tomorrow."
"Really?" asked Hannah.
The gorilla nodded and smiled.
  The next morning Hannah woke up and saw the toy gorilla.
She smiled.

Hannah rushed downstairs to tell her father what had happened.
"Happy birthday, love," he said. "Do you want to go to the zoo?"
Hannah looked at him.

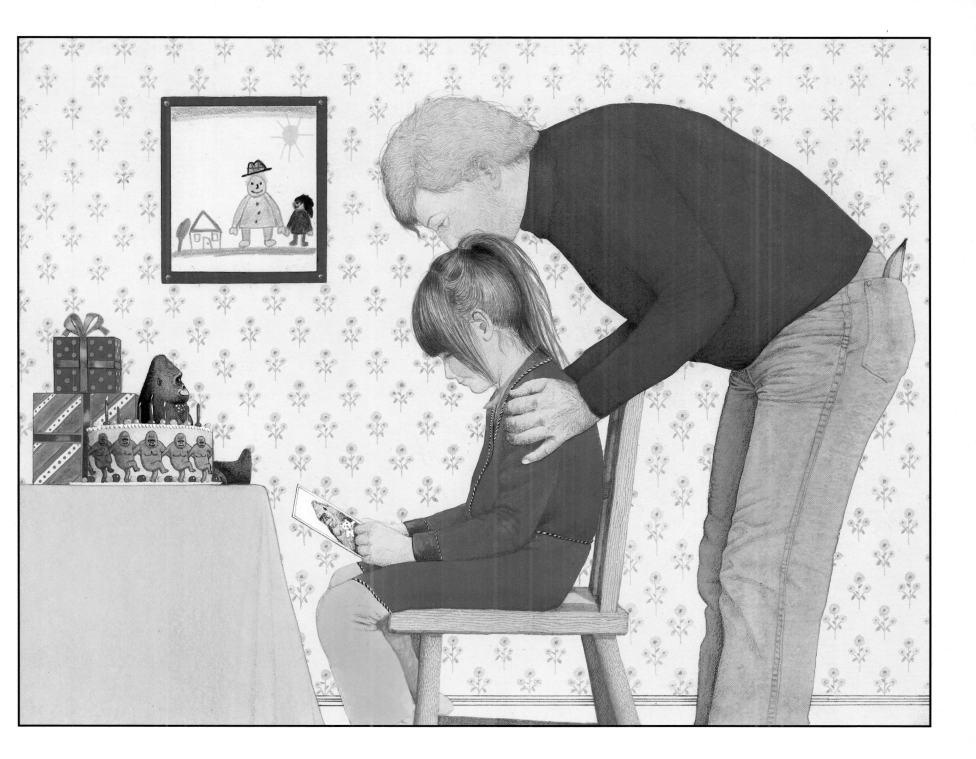

She was very happy.